D1239176

Because You Are

Because You Are

Jael Richardson

illustrated by Nneka Myers

HarperCollinsPublishersLtd

Because You Are
Text copyright © 2022 by Jael Richardson.
Illustrations copyright © 2022 by Nneka Myers.
All rights reserved.

Published by HarperCollins Publishers Ltd

No part of this book may be used or reproduced in any manner
whatsoever without the prior written permission of the publisher,
except in the case of brief quotations embodied in reviews.

HarperCollins books may be purchased for educational, business or
sales promotional use through our Special Markets Department.

HarperCollins Publishers Ltd
Bay Adelaide Centre, East Tower
22 Adelaide Street West, 41st Floor
Toronto, Ontario, Canada
M5H 4E3

www.harpercollins.ca

Library and Archives Canada Cataloguing in Publication

Title: Because you are / Jael Richardson ; illustrated by Nneka Myers.
Names: Richardson, Jael Ealey, 1980- author. | Myers, Nneka, illustrator.
Identifiers: Canadiana (print) 20220189951 | Canadiana (ebook) 2022018996X
ISBN 9781443464802 (hardcover) | ISBN 9781443464819 (ebook)
Classification: LCC PS8635.I33345 B43 2022 | DDC jC813/.6—dc23

Printed and bound in the United States of America

PHX 9 8 7 6 5 4 3 2 1

For Reina. —JR

For Dora Myers, my beloved mommy. —NM

Little one,
there's something you should know.

You are just right
just enough
as you are.

More than that,
you are a marvel,
a delight.

You are the shape
of a million dreams of greatness
that form a powerful work of art.

You are
loved by your ancestors,
who hoped for you
and longed for you
and here
you are.

But there's something I need to tell you, something I need you to know.

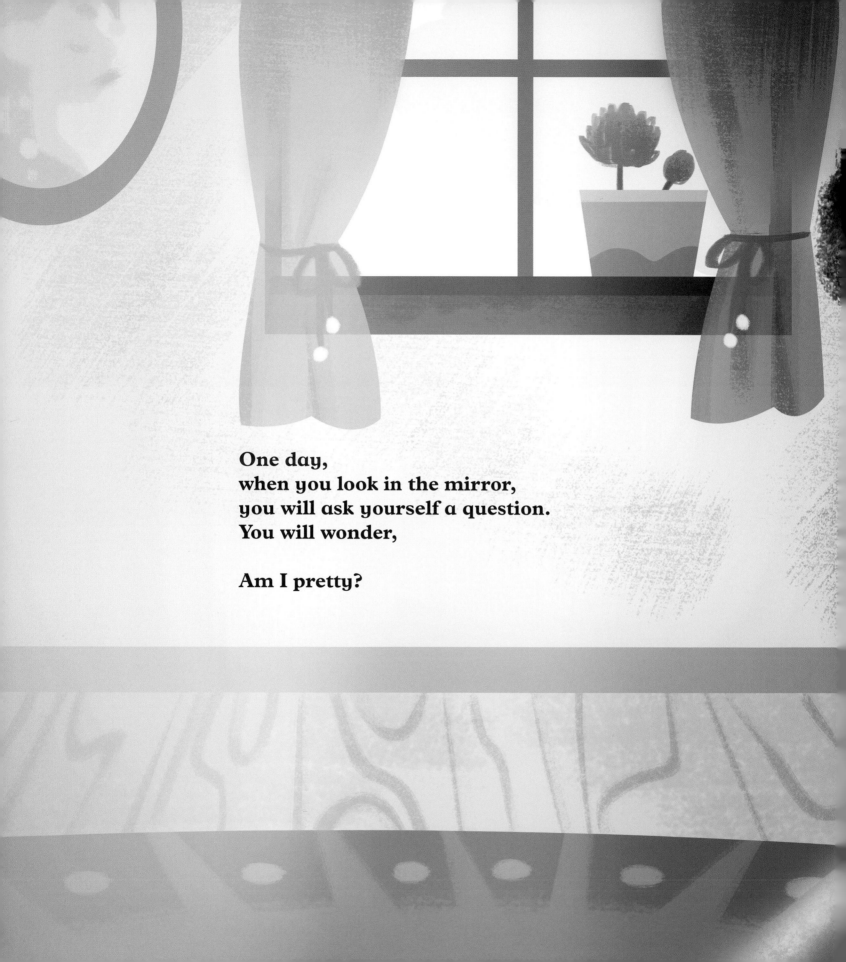

One day,
when you look in the mirror,
you will ask yourself a question.
You will wonder,

Am I pretty?

Pretty.

It's a word you'll hear a lot—
said to you
or around you
or about someone else.

She's so pretty.

You'll tilt your head
and think about
what it might look like
to be pretty.

"Am I pretty?" you'll whisper in the mirror,
full of worry and wonder.

But pretty is just a word.

A sometimes word,
an outside word,
that's used
and overused
to describe things
people see
with only their eyes.

Don't you look pretty today in that picture
in that dress
with that bow
with that hair
in those shoes
with that crown on your head.

"You look so pretty," they say.

But what you think
and what you say
mean so much more
than what people see
with their eyes.

What you think
and what you say
and what you do for others
add beauty to the world.

And beautiful
is a big and brilliant word.

So think beautiful thoughts and do beautiful things.

Love your neighbour,
be generous,
help others,
fight for what's right wherever
and however
you can.

Be beautiful, little one.

Because what you do
and how you do it
can change
your family
your school
your neighbourhood
your country
your world.

And
that
is
beautiful—
to make the world
just a little bit better wherever you are.

You are a story that's worth being written
and read
and lived proudly.
So get to it.
Start now.
Dream big.

Every day
and always,
be
beautiful.

Because you are.